This art was created with watercolors, ink, and oil sticks.

Another Important Book
Text copyright © 1999 by Roberta Brown Rauch
Illustrations copyright © 1999 by Chris Raschka
Manufactured in China. All rights reserved. No part of this book may be used or
reproduced in any manner whatsoever without written permission except in the case of
brief quotations embodied in critical articles and reviews. For information address
HarperCollins Children's Books, a division of HarperCollins Publishers,
195 Broadway, New York, NY 10007.
www.harperchildrens.com

Library of Congress Cataloging-in-Publication Data
Brown, Margaret Wise.
    Another important book / by Margaret Wise Brown ; pictures by Chris Raschka.
        p.   cm.
    "Joanna Cotler books."
    Summary: Illustrations and simple rhyming text describe how a child grows from
ages one through six.
    ISBN-10: 0-06-026282-6 (trade bdg.) — ISBN-13: 978-0-06-026282-2 (trade bdg.)
    ISBN-10: 0-06-026283-4 (lib. bdg.) — ISBN-13: 978-0-06-026283-9 (lib. bdg.)
    ISBN-10: 0-06-443785-X (pbk.) — ISBN-13: 978-0-06-443785-1 (pbk.)
    [1. Growth—Fiction.   2. Stories in rhyme.]   I. Raschka, Christopher, ill.   II. Title.
Pz8.3.B815An   1999   98-7212
[E]—dc21   CIP
                                                                                                AC

Typography by Alicia Mikles
14 15 16 SCP 20 19 18 17 16

For Sam, Ahna, James, Ezra,
Catherine, Ingo, Madeline, Solveig,
and Eliana Matea
—C.R.

Another IMPORTANT BOOK

BY MARGARET WISE BROWN

PICTURES BY CHRIS RASCHKA

JOANNA COTLER BOOKS

An Imprint of HarperCollinsPublishers

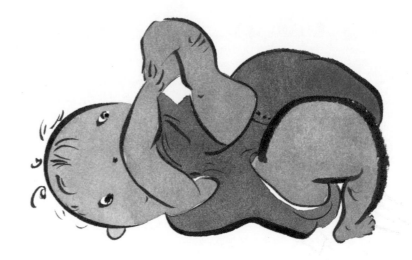

The important thing
about being One
is that life
has just begun.

You can't quite talk.

You can't quite walk.

You've found your nose

and discovered your toes.

You've seen the moon

and felt the sun.

But the important thing about being One
is that life has just begun.

The important thing about being Two
is all the things that you can do.

You can walk, talk
and sneeze and wheeze
and laugh and tease
and cough and dance
and jump and prance
and cry and run
and have some fun.

And the important thing about being Two
is all the things that you can do.

The important thing about being Three
is being ME.

Who is it that can open their eyes and see?

ME!

Who knows the difference between a pig and a tree?

ME!

Who runs around as busy as a bee?

ME!

Who is funny and not a bunny?

ME!

But the important thing about being Three
is being ME.

The important thing about being Four
is that you are bigger than you were before.

Now at Four,
you can open the door.
You've grown a lot,
you'll grow some more.
You can blink and think
as quick as a wink.

You can open your eyes

to a world of surprise.

You can run and race
everywhere.

You can sing and fling
your arms in the air.

But the important thing about being Four
is that you are bigger than you were before.

The important thing about Five and Six

is that you learn a lot of tricks.

You learn how to count.

You learn how to read.

You know how to dress

and get what you need.

You can almost tell time.

You can speak in rhyme.

But the important thing about Five and Six
is that you learn a lot of tricks.

Each day you grow a little more.

Each day you're older than before.

At One your life has just begun.

At Two there's so much you can do.

At Three you discover ME.

At Four you're bigger than you were before.

At Five and Six you learn some tricks.

But the important

thing about

Six

Five

Four

Three

One

and

Two

is that you

are

YOU.